Farmyard Tales

Barn on Fire

Heather Amery

Illustrated by Stephen Cartwright

Adapted by Lara Bryan

Reading consultant: Alison Kelly

Find the duck on every double page.

This story is about Apple Tree Farm,

Sam,   Poppy,

Mrs.
Boot,  Ted,

some fire fighters,

and Rusty.

It was a busy morning
on the farm.

Poppy and Sam were
helping Ted fix a fence.

Rusty sniffed. He had spotted something.

"Smoke," said Ted. "Something's burning."

"The barn must be on fire!" cried Poppy.

"Run home as fast as you can," said Ted.

Ted ran to the barn.

"The hay barn is on fire," shouted Poppy.

Mrs. Boot called the number for the fire fighters.

"Please come quickly."

Soon, they heard the fire truck's siren.

"Please stay in the house," Mrs. Boot told Poppy and Sam.

"The fire is at the hay barn," she told the fire fighters.

The fire fighters jumped
out of the truck.

They brought
out the hoses.

They pumped water
from the pond.

Squawk!

Poppy and Sam
watched the water
squirt over the barn.

That should put
the fire out.

But the barn was
still burning.

One of the fire fighters
ran to look behind
the barn.

"What a surprise!"
he said.

"The barn isn't on fire."

Two campers were
cooking on a campfire.

The fire went out.

Everyone was safe...

...and Rusty had an early lunch.

PUZZLES

Puzzle 1

Put the five pictures in order.

A.

B.

C.

D.

E.

23

Puzzle 2

Look at the picture and count the:

fire fighters 5

hoses 4

ducks 2 duck

Puzzle 3

Can you spot the five differences between these two pictures?

Puzzle 4

Find these things in the picture:

water   wood   smoke
helmets   dog   pan   sausages

Puzzle 5

Fill in the missing word.

fire   ~~morning~~   ~~water~~   home

A.  It was a busy
<u>morning</u>.

B.  Run <u>home</u>!

C.  They pumped
<u>water</u>.

D.  The <u>fire</u>
went out.

Answers to puzzles
Puzzle 1

barn must be fired cried poppy

The hay barn is on fire shout poppy

1D.

2A.

3C.

4E.

5B.

28

Puzzle 2

There are <u>five</u> fire fighters.
There are <u>four</u> hoses.
There are <u>two</u> ducks.

Puzzle 3

Puzzle 4

helmets

smoke

wood

dog

sausages

pan

water

Puzzle 5

A. It was a busy <u>morning</u>.

B. Run <u>home</u>!

C. They pumped <u>water</u>.

D. The <u>fire</u> went out.

Designed by Laura Nelson
Digital manipulation by
Nick Wakeford and John Russell

This edition first published in 2017 by Usborne Publishing Ltd.,
Usborne House, 83-85 Saffron Hill, London EC1N 8RT, England.
www.usborne.com Copyright © 2017, 1990 Usborne Publishing Ltd.

USBORNE FIRST READING
Level Two

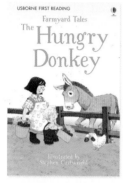

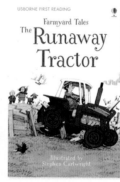

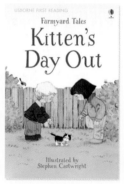

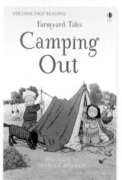